D0316504

This Oscar book
belongs to:

....

....

....

First published 2006 by Walker Books Ltd
87 Vauxhall Walk, London SE11 5HJ

This edition published 2007

10 9 8 7 6 5 4 3 2 1

This book has been typeset in ITCKabel

Printed in China

British Library Cataloguing in Publication Data: a catalogue
record for this book is available from the British Library

ISBN 978-1-4063-0497-8

www.walkerbooks.co.uk

WALKER BOOKS
AND SUBSIDIARIES
LONDON · BOSTON · SYDNEY · AUCKLAND

For
Charlotte
and Lauren
G.W.

The author and publisher would like to thank Sue Ellis at
the Centre for Literacy in Primary Education, Martin Jenkins
and Paul Harrison for their invaluable input and guidance
during the making of this book.

OSCAR and the CRICKET

A BOOK ABOUT MOVING AND ROLLING

Geoff Waring

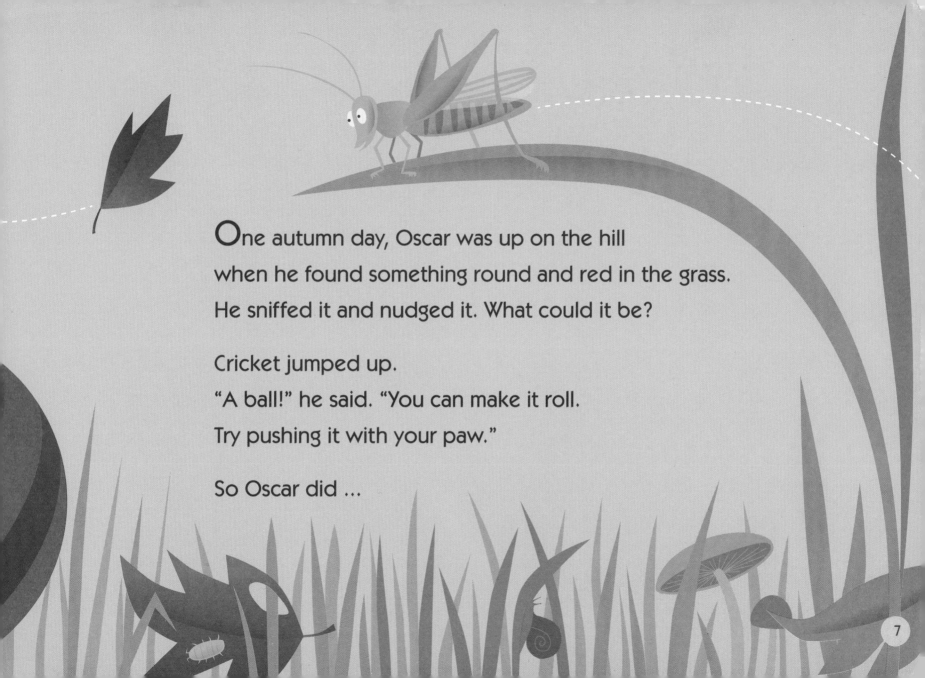

One autumn day, Oscar was up on the hill
when he found something round and red in the grass.
He sniffed it and nudged it. What could it be?

Cricket jumped up.
"A ball!" he said. "You can make it roll.
Try pushing it with your paw."

So Oscar did ...

and the ball rolled away through the grass ...

then lay still.

"Why has it stopped?" Oscar asked.

"The thick grass slowed it down," Cricket said.

"Try rolling it on the path."

But a long branch was lying in the way.

"We'll have to move it," Cricket said.

"I'm not big or strong enough,

but you are, Oscar. Try giving it a pull."

"Uuuuurgh," Oscar groaned.

Slowly the branch started to move.

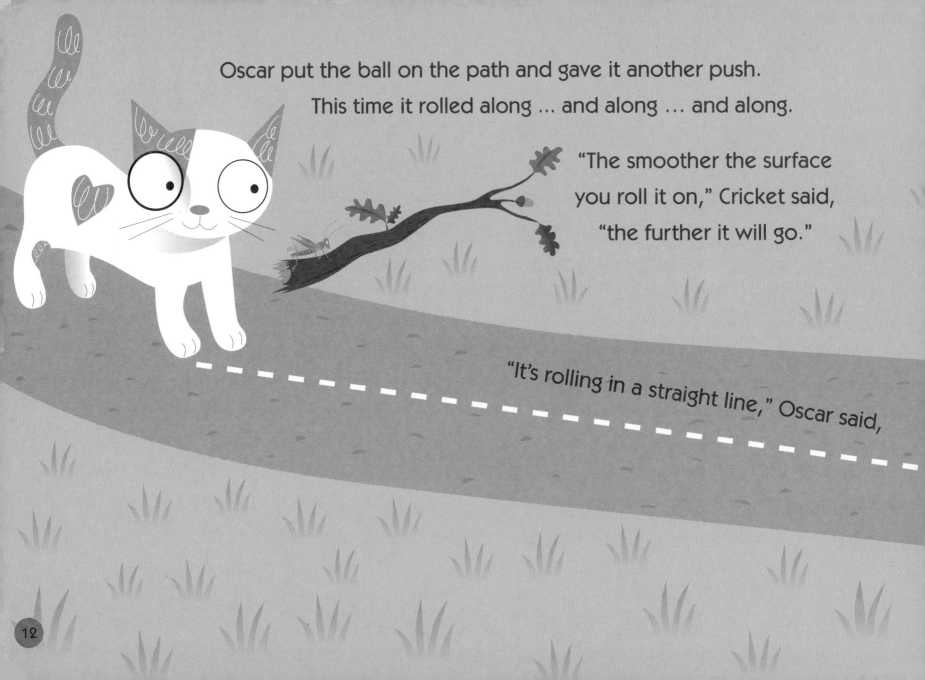

Oscar put the ball on the path and gave it another push.
This time it rolled along ... and along ... and along.

"The smoother the surface
you roll it on," Cricket said,
"the further it will go."

"It's rolling in a straight line," Oscar said,

"and it's heading towards …

... the tree!"

"Oh dear!" Oscar said.
"It's alright," said Cricket.
"The ball hit the side
of the tree, and that set it
rolling in a different direction."

BOUNCE!

For a moment, Oscar stopped watching the ball to look up. All the leaves were swaying and fluttering.

"They can move
by themselves!" Oscar said.
"It looks like it," Cricket said,
"but the wind is pushing them
and making them move."

17

"Does everything need a push to make it move?" Oscar asked. "What about me?"

"You can move by yourself," Cricket said. "Most animals can. Our bodies have muscles to help us."

And he jumped up

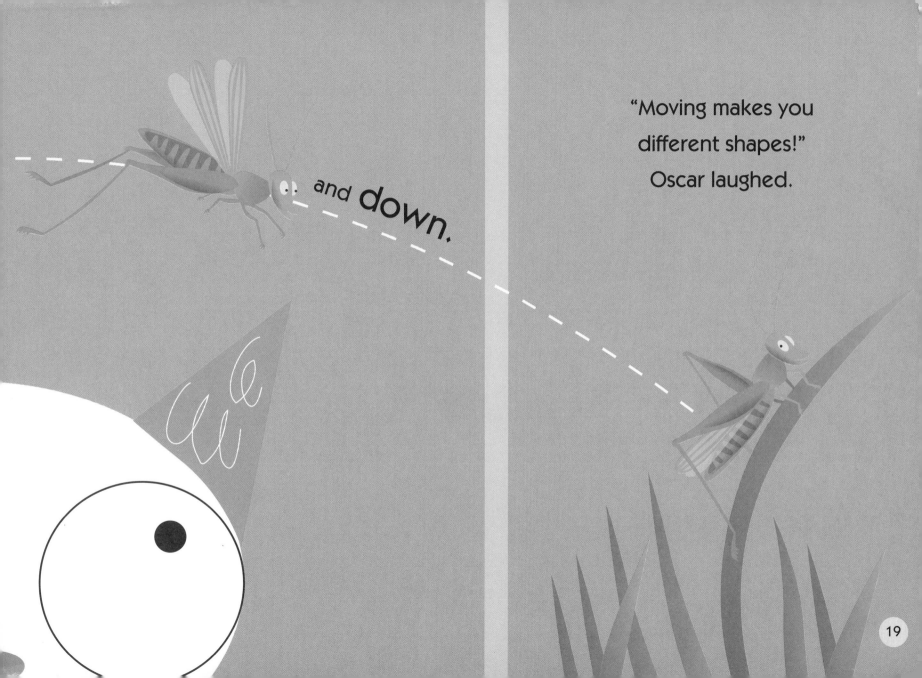

...and down.

"Moving makes you different shapes!" Oscar laughed.

"We can use our muscles to move ourselves and to move other things too," Cricket said.

A leaf cutter ant can lift fifty times its own body weight in its jaws.

A hawfinch can crack a hard cherry stone in its bill.

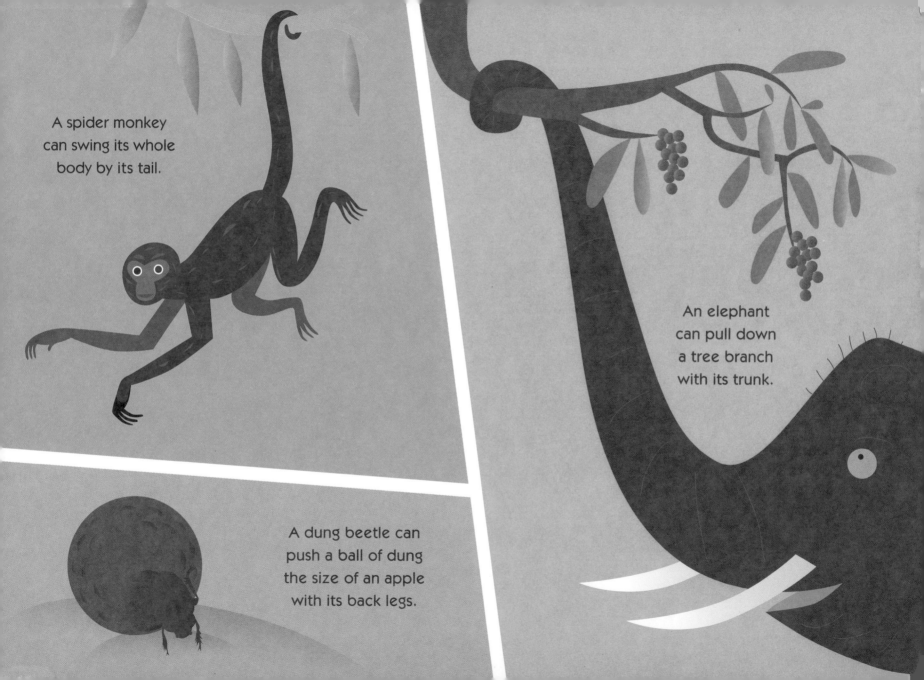

A spider monkey can swing its whole body by its tail.

A dung beetle can push a ball of dung the size of an apple with its back legs.

An elephant can pull down a tree branch with its trunk.

Just then Oscar saw the ball again, lying in the grass. This time he gave it a great BIG push.

and it rolled through a leafy bit.

It rolled through a muddy bit,

"It's slowing down," Oscar said.

"Yes," Cricket said. "But it hasn't stopped.

You gave it such a strong push."

"Perhaps it will never stop!"
Oscar said.

But just then,
a kitten put out a paw
and stopped the ball.

"Hello," said Oscar. "I'm Oscar
and this is Cricket. Who are you?"

"Ted," said Ted.
"Can I play?"

25

Ted gave the ball a push.
Oscar ran after it.
"Look out!" called Cricket.

Run!

Flutter!

Roll!

Jump!

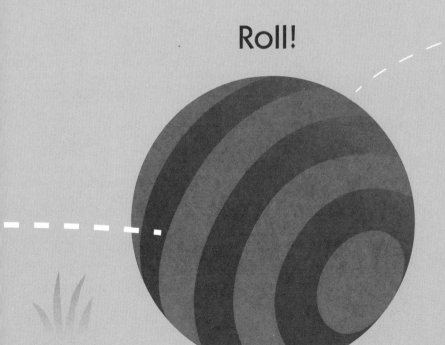

Everything was moving
on the hill.

Thinking some more about moving and rolling

On the hill, Oscar found out about these things...

Getting going

An object needs an outside force – a push
or a pull – to start it moving.

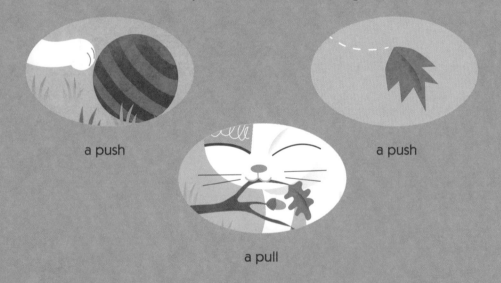

a push

a push

a pull

Try moving different objects. Which ones can you push?
Which ones can you pull? Are there some you can push *and* pull?

Keeping going

Once an object is moving it travels
in a straight line, unless something
gets in the way.

bounce

See if you can make something move
in two directions – try up and down
or forwards and backwards.

Stopping

An object needs an outside force to stop it moving too.

The stronger the force, the more quickly it stops.

stopping after a
short time

stopping after a
long time

stopping instantly

Try pushing a ball on a smooth surface and on a bumpy surface.

What do you notice?

Oscar thinks moving and rolling are great! Do you too?

OSCAR and the FROG
A BOOK ABOUT GROWING

Geoff Waring

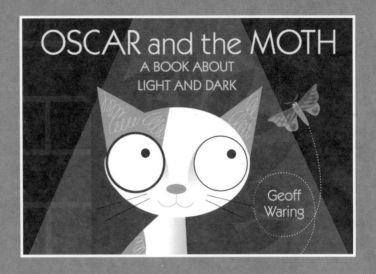

OSCAR and the MOTH
A BOOK ABOUT
LIGHT AND DARK

Geoff Waring

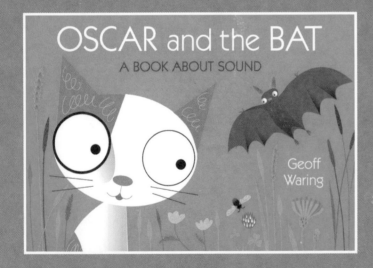

OSCAR and the BAT
A BOOK ABOUT SOUND

Geoff Waring

OSCAR and the CRICKET
A BOOK ABOUT MOVING
AND ROLLING

Geoff Waring

Which of these Oscar books have you read?